TOM PALMER

FOOTBALL ACADEMY

BOYS UNITED

Illustrated by
Brian Williamson

PUFFIN

PUFFIN BOOKS

Published by the Penguin Group
Penguin Books Ltd, 80 Strand, London WC2R ORL, England
Penguin Group (USA) Inc., 375 Hudson Street, New York, New York 10014, USA
Penguin Group (Canada), 90 Eglinton Avenue East, Suite 700, Toronto, Ontario, Canada M4P 2Y3
(a division of Pearson Penguin Canada Inc.)
Penguin Ireland, 25 St Stephen's Green, Dublin 2, Ireland (a division of Penguin Books Ltd)
Penguin Group (Australia), 250 Camberwell Road, Camberwell, Victoria 3124, Australia
(a division of Pearson Australia Group Pty Ltd)
Penguin Books India Pvt Ltd, 11 Community Centre, Panchsheel Park, New Delhi – 110 017, India
Penguin Group (NZ), 67 Apollo Drive, Rosedale, North Shore 0632, New Zealand
(a division of Pearson New Zealand Ltd)
Penguin Books (South Africa) (Pty) Ltd, 24 Sturdee Avenue, Rosebank, Johannesburg 2196, South Africa

Penguin Books Ltd, Registered Offices: 80 Strand, London WC2R ORL, England

puffinbooks.com

First published 2009

024

Text copyright © Tom Palmer, 2009
Illustrations copyright © Brian Williamson, 2009
All rights reserved

The moral right of the author and illustrator has been asserted

Set in 14.5/21 pt Baskerville MT
Typeset by Palimpsest Book Production Limited, Grangemouth, Stirlingshire
Made and printed in England by Clays Ltd, Elcograf S.p.A.

British Library Cataloguing in Publication Data
A CIP catalogue record for this book is available from the British Library

ISBN: 978-0-141-32467-8

www.greenpenguin.co.uk

MIX
Paper from
responsible sources
FSC
www.fsc.org   FSC® C018179

Penguin Books is committed to a sustainable
future for our business, our readers and our planet.
This book is made from Forest Stewardship
Council™ certified paper.

BOYS UNITED

...m Palmer is a football fan and a writer. He ...ver did well at school. But once he got into ...ading about football – in newspapers, ...gazines and books – he decided he wanted ...e a football writer more than anything. As ... as the Football Academy series, he is the ...hor of the Football Detective series, also ... Puffin Books.

Tom lives in a Yorkshire town called ...lmorden with his wife and daughter. The ...t stadium he's visited is Real Madrid's ...ntiago Bernabéu.

Find out more about Tom on his website *tompalmer.co.uk*

Books by Tom Palmer

FOOTBALL ACADEMY: BOYS UNITED
FOOTBALL ACADEMY: STRIKING OUT

For older readers

FOOTBALL DETECTIVE: FOUL PLAY

For Peter, wish you were here too

Contents

Jake

Ever since he could walk, Jake Oldfield had played football. And ever since he could *remember*, he had dreamed of being a professional footballer. Not because he wanted to be rich and famous like Steven Gerrard or Wayne Rooney. It wasn't that. He wanted to be a footballer because he *loved* football.

If football could be his *job*, that would be great.

He didn't want to go to a boring office

every morning like his mum. Or to a
factory like his dad. Both of them indoors
all day. Jake wanted to be on football
pitches: running, tackling and scoring
goals.

Jake collected the ball in midfield and
looked up.

There was no one from his village team
ahead of him. Nor at the side of him. Just

three defenders from the other team, then the keeper and the goal.

It was down to Jake to win this game.

When the first defender approached, Jake waited for him to come really close, then tapped the ball forward, sprinting past him.

One down, two to go.

The second defender came clattering forward, lunging into Jake at full speed. But Jake just sidestepped him and the defender ended up on his backside in a muddy puddle.

Two down, one to go.

The third defender was standing perfectly still. Waiting.

Jake had tried to get past him several times already during the match. But this defender was quick and had whipped the ball off Jake's feet, whether Jake put it to his left or to his right.

So this time . . . Jake chipped him.

For a second the defender didn't know what to do. He just stood there.

And a second was all Jake needed. With the ball in the air, he ran past the last defender and into the penalty area. And as the ball came down, Jake hammered it towards the top left corner of the goal.

The keeper dived. But it was no use. The ball was in the back of the net before he hit the ground, and Jake was wheeling away to celebrate his winner.

After the game, the team manager came over.

'That, Jake, was the best goal you've ever scored for us.'

'Thanks, Mr Newbrook,' Jake said.

'It's a shame it might be your last,' his manager said.

Jake looked down at his feet. He didn't know what to say.

'It's the trial at United this week, isn't it?' Mr Newbrook said.

'In two days,' said Jake. It was all he'd been able to think about for days. 'I'm sorry.'

Mr Newbrook laughed. 'Don't be sorry, Jake. We're all *thrilled* for you. If you get a place at United, it'll be one of the best things that has happened in this village. You're one of only two players to make it into a professional club – let alone the Premiership.'

Jake looked at his team-mates who had gathered at the side of the pitch. If he *did* get a place at United he wouldn't be allowed to play for this team any more. Only for United. And that made him sad. But the idea of being a United player made him happier.

'Get some practice in with your dad the

rest of this week, Jake,' Mr Newbrook said. 'Make sure you're sharp.'

Jake looked over at his dad, who was standing at the side of the pitch. Dad gave him a thumbs up.

'I will,' Jake said, turning to Mr Newbrook again.

'And Jake?'

'Yeah?'

'Just remember that it's what *kind* of player you are that matters. Not whether you're tall or small.'

Jake smiled. Mr Newbrook had read his mind.

The trial at United wasn't Jake's first.

He had tried out at City, Bolton and Blackburn before. But every time he got that far, he was told that he was a very good player . . . but that he was too small to make it.

'I will, Mr Newbrook,' Jake said. 'And thanks.'

'You're welcome,' Mr Newbrook said. 'Go and make us proud.'

Too Small for Football

The next day Dad took Jake to the library.

'What are we doing here?' Jake asked. 'It's the trial tomorrow. Can't we go and practise?'

'Later,' Dad said. 'We need to look at some books first.'

Jake was puzzled. What was going on?

Dad had always trained him – ever since he could remember. And not just for an ordinary kick about.

He'd have Jake running at speed on and off the ball.

Heading, sprinting, tackling.

Blocking, passing.

Everything.

So what were they doing in the library, standing next to a huge *Back to School* display?

Then Jake got it. Dad was thinking about school. Not football. The new academic year was about to start – in three days. And it wasn't just a new school year: it was a new *school*. High school.

The new school had been on Jake's mind. But only the back of his mind. He'd been more worried about the trial at United, so his school nerves had barely registered.

But he realized he'd have to face it now. School. Books. And his dad was making sure he took it seriously.

'Right,' Dad said. 'Where are the football books?'

'In the children's section,' Jake replied, surprised. This wasn't what he'd expected.

He led his dad over.

'These are good,' Dad said, looking through a dozen books about playing the game: how to attack, defend or be a keeper. 'But what about biographies?'

'I don't know about them,' Jake said.

A woman putting books out turned to face Jake and his dad.

'Biography is over there,' she said, pointing.

'Thanks.'

Dad scanned the biography section, pulling off three books. Biographies of footballers called Kevin Keegan, Alan Ball and David Batty. Jake had heard of one of them – Kevin Keegan – his dad's favourite footballer from years ago. Dad had a signed photo of him in the front room at home.

'How are these going to help, Dad? Let's just go and play football.'

'Just a minute,' Dad said. 'I want you to see them.' He opened the books at the pictures, showing each of the players in a team photograph.

'What have they all got in common?' Dad asked.

'I don't know,' Jake said.

'Look again,' Dad said.

'At what?'

'They're small.'

'What?'

'They're all small players,' Dad said.

Jake looked at the pictures again. The three players Dad had pointed out were smaller than all of their team-mates. Much smaller.

Dad leafed to the backs of the books, where each footballer's playing record was listed. All the games they'd played for club and country. All the goals they'd scored. All the awards they'd won.

'Between them,' Dad said, pointing at the pages again, 'these three have played for England nearly two hundred times. They've won World Cups, Premierships, European Footballer of the Year awards. And when they were young they were all told they were too small to make it. But they all *did* make it!'

Now Jake understood why his dad had brought him to the library.

The Manager

Jake was nervous.

Nervous, because the gateway his dad had just driven him through was the entrance to United's training ground – and to United's famous Academy for young players. Dad had always said that nerves were part of the body's preparation. That Jake needed to be full of nervous energy or he wouldn't play well at the times it really mattered.

Jake glanced at his dad.

Dad smiled back.

'Good thing we haven't got any City stickers on the car,' Dad said.

Jake smiled. He'd tried not to think about the fact that he was a City fan – entering the territory of the enemy, United.

They were now driving up a long narrow road. It was more like the approach to a stately home than a football training-ground. On one side there was a long line of trees, all exactly the same distance apart. On the other, a massive garden sweeping up a hill.

It wasn't at all what Jake had been expecting. He'd thought it'd be all modern, made of glass and steel, like the new buildings at his old school. But the Academy was built within the old buildings of what must have been a place where *seriously* posh people used to live. The dressing rooms were in what probably used to be the stables. The pitches were part of the grounds.

And if you looked carefully through the trees, you could see the old house. As big as a football stadium, with dozens of chimneys.

Some of the pitches Jake could see were grass and some were all-weather. He checked for players training. This was the place where six of England's current squad had learned to play football from the age of eight – three years younger than Jake was now. He could bump into any of them here: it was where they still trained.

Half an hour later, Jake was standing patiently with fifteen other boys at the side of the pitch – all ready for the trial.

Some of them were kitted out in United gear; others in plain tops.

'Right, lads,' said the man who was running the session. 'I am Steve Cooper, manager of the under-twelves here at United. You can call me Steve. Let's get started.'

Steve was a muscular man of medium height with dark straggly hair. He reminded Jake of the men he'd seen in war films: leaders, barking out orders. His voice was deep and broad.

'We're going to go through a set of exercises,' Steve said. 'To look at your pace. To look at your skills. To look at your character. Then we're going to have a short game. Eight-a-side. We'll be here about two hours in all. OK?'

All the boys nodded.

Jake gazed across to the other side of the pitch to where the parents were standing, a row of twenty or twenty-five of them. He saw his dad looking back at him, smiling. The sun broke through a cloud and the Academy was suddenly warm and bright.

Yunis

fter warming up with two laps of
the pitch – running forwards,
backwards and sidewards – the trial
moved on to sprinting. Jake was the fastest;
an Asian lad close behind him.

As he looked at the manager making
notes on his clipboard, the Asian lad came
up to Jake. He was tall and broad-
shouldered with short dark hair.

'You're fast,' he said to Jake.

'So are you,' Jake said.

'Thanks. I'm Yunis.'

'I'm Jake.'

'I'm glad we started with running,' Yunis said. 'I feel better now.'

'Me too,' Jake said, looking over at the manager again. 'It makes you feel more confident, doesn't it? That we've done well at something already.'

'Yeah,' Yunis said. 'What position do you play anyway? You're not a striker, are you?'

'No. Left wing. How about you?'

'Striker.'

'Right.' Jake smiled. That was good: it meant they weren't in competition with each other for the same place.

Yunis looked across at the parents who were all standing five metres from the pitch, behind a line that they weren't allowed to cross.

'Is your dad there?' Yunis asked.

'Yeah. The one on the end. In the grey jacket,' Jake said. 'Which is yours?'

'He's not here.'

'Couldn't he make it?' Jake asked.

'He could,' Yunis said. 'But he doesn't want to. He thinks football's a waste of time.'

Jake shrugged, making Yunis smile.

'I know!' Yunis said. 'Like *football* is a waste of time!'

For the next hour the boys were asked to dribble round cones, hit one-touch passes to each other, take dead balls, throw-ins and try to tackle.

By now Jake was feeling confident. But he knew it was when the game started that he would have the chance to shine. In the game he could run with the ball and cross it into the box. The thing he liked to do best.

Jake was put in left midfield for the eight-a-side, his favourite position. He was up against a huge right-sided full-back. The first time Jake called for the ball it was played to his feet. He took it to the edge of the pitch to beat the defender on the outside, but the defender closed him down and barged him off the ball.

A shoulder-charge.

Jake picked himself up, glancing at the manager, Steve Cooper. He was making more notes.

Who was he writing about? And what was he writing?

The next time Jake got the ball he tried to take it round the big defender again. But he was tackled hard again, and he lost the ball.

He looked at the manager, then at Dad. Jake felt he'd been fouled. But he knew not

to make anything of it. If the manager
didn't think it was a foul, then it wasn't a
foul.

Jake knew what Steve Cooper was
thinking: that boy's barged off the ball easily
– he's *too small*.

His heart sank.

It was happening again.

Everything was going wrong.

Goal!

Jake looked over at Dad. He needed help if this trial was going to get any better. He was losing his confidence. Fast.

Dad was holding his hands flat at the side of his eyes, like a horse's blinkers. Jake knew immediately what he meant: focus, forget about the manager with the clipboard, play your natural game.

What had Dad said yesterday at the library? About those three short players.

That they'd all played for England. They'd won World Cups. Everything. And they were all told they were too small to make it. But they did make it.

It helped remembering what Dad had said.

So the next time the ball came to Jake, he knocked it quickly to Yunis and sprinted past the big defender. The defender tried to lunge at him, but Jake skipped over his legs.

Then Yunis played it back to Jake. And suddenly Jake was in loads of space.

But he took his time. He was aware he'd wrong-footed the big full-back and that he didn't need to rush. He ran towards the goal and did a Ronaldo step-over to beat the next defender. Then he slid the ball to Yunis, who'd run into the box.

Yunis met the ball with his right foot.

One–nil.

Jake heard applause from the manager behind him. But he didn't look round. He just took up his position for the restart.

'That was great, Jake,' Yunis said. 'Thank you!'

'No worries.' Jake smiled. 'Good goal. From now on, once I've beaten the first defender, I'll try and get an early cross into the box for you. OK?'

'Suits me! Cheers, Jake.' Yunis was grinning.

The game went well from then.

Somehow the big defender wasn't getting near Jake now. And Yunis was the perfect striker, always in the right place at the right time.

Jake set Yunis up with three more goals, all crosses from the left.

And, with a minute of the practice game to go, Jake decided to show he could shoot too. Instead of playing the ball in to Yunis, Jake dummied a pass, sending both defenders with the striker, then drew the keeper off his line and chipped him.

Goal. A beauty.

Jake heard Dad shout a loud 'YES'. He looked over at him and smiled.

Then he noticed a man standing near Dad, wearing a long overcoat. The man was clapping. He looked *really* familiar. But Jake couldn't quite place him.

He must be another boy's father, Jake thought. Someone he'd seen at the football before, maybe.

'Who's that in the long coat?' Jake said, as Yunis jogged beside him.

'Don't you know?' Yunis replied, looking surprised.

Jake didn't have time to answer. Steve had blown his whistle. The game was over.

'Right, lads,' Steve said. 'You all did well. As you know, we can only take two – maybe three – players on for next season. So, you go and get those kits off. We'll make our decision and talk to our choices individually.'

Sixteen boys walked off to the dressing rooms, aware that two or three of their lives might be about to change for ever.

They Think It's All Over

Jake was sitting with his head down, trying to relax after the trial. When he looked up from his kitbag, Yunis was standing over him.

'I thought you'd gone,' Jake said.

Yunis shook his head, but said nothing.

He was in a school blazer and black trousers. He looked smart. A bit out of place among the other lads who were wearing Nike, Bench and Adidas.

'I wanted to say thanks,' Yunis said

eventually, his voice stumbling. 'For all the crosses and that.'

'That's all right,' Jake said. 'You were good for me too.'

'But listen . . . I just went outside . . .' Yunis stopped again.

'Are you OK?' Jake asked.

Yunis spoke quietly, leaning towards Jake. '. . . and they've asked me to sign schoolboy forms.'

Jake stood up. Yunis was now a United player. Under-twelves, maybe. But a United player all the same.

'That's great,' Jake said. 'I'm really pleased for you.'

'It's down to you. I owe you.' Yunis put his hand out.

Jake shook it. 'You're welcome,' he said.

'I've got to go,' Yunis said, looking at his watch. 'My dad's waiting for me.'

'Did he come after all? That's great.'

'No. He's not *here*. He'll be at the end of the drive, checking his watch.'

'But won't he be happy – that you've got a place?'

'No. He'll be gutted. But my mum got him to let me come. As long as I keep up with my school stuff. That's the deal.'

Jake didn't know what to say. He felt a bit sorry for Yunis that no one had been there to share his moment of glory.

'I'd better go,' Yunis said. 'I hope you get in too. I bet you do. See you later.'

'See you,' Jake said.

He watched Yunis leave and felt glad his dad was with him, whether he got picked or not.

The minute Yunis had gone through the door, a man burst into the dressing rooms,

31

red in the face. He was wearing tracksuit bottoms with an England badge on the leg.

'WILL! WILL! YOU'RE IN,' he shouted.

He ran past Jake straight to his son – a boy with short blond hair – and lifted him off the ground. The boy looked confused. His dad roared like a goal had been scored. Except he was the only one roaring. Everyone else was quiet.

'I said "Yes", of course. The forms are there to sign. You're a United player!'

The dad stared at the other boys, grinning at them. Then he led his son out of the dressing rooms.

Those left behind looked at each other for a few seconds, then at the floor. They all knew that it was over. Once they stepped outside the dressing rooms they'd be told – by their dad or their mum – that they'd not made it.

One of the boys kicked his kitbag across the dressing room.

Jake closed his eyes. He felt like crying. He had failed at a trial.

Again.

The Famous
Frenchman

A few minutes later, Steve Cooper came into the dressing room. Most of the boys were ready now, but there were bags and kits strewn all over the place. No one had said anything since the loud dad had been in.

'OK,' Steve said. 'Just to let you know that we've spoken to the parents we need to. And the boys, I think.'

He looked around the room to check, Jake assumed, that Will and Yunis weren't

34

there any more. Jake tried to catch his eye –
to say thank you. But Steve hadn't seen
Jake.

'And we've chosen the players we
want.' Steve paused. 'I'm sorry that you
lot haven't made it this time. Once you're
outside we'll give you a bit of feedback on
why we didn't go with you, and what you
can do to up your chances next time.
OK?'

Some of the lads nodded. Jake looked up at the manager, but he still hadn't noticed him.

Jake felt numb. Like he didn't care if he'd been picked or not.

Outside the dressing rooms it felt cold. The sun had gone in. The training fields looked grey. Jake scanned the crowd of parents and boys for Dad. He couldn't see him. But he did see someone else. And he couldn't quite believe it.

It was the United manager. The *first* team manager. The famous Frenchman who was forever arguing with interviewers on *Match of the Day*. The man in the overcoat he'd seen when he'd been playing in the trial. He hadn't recognized him from a distance.

Jake had never seen him in the flesh, so

he couldn't help but stare. Until he noticed the Frenchman and Steve were staring back at him, smiling. *With* Jake's dad.

Jake's dad gestured to him, but Jake stood still, rooted to the spot. So Dad turned to the first team manager, shook his hand vigorously and began to walk over to Jake.

It was only when Dad got nearer, that Jake noticed he had tears in his eyes.

At first Dad couldn't speak. But eventually he cleared his throat. 'They want you,' Dad said.

'What?'

'They want you,' Dad repeated, 'to sign schoolboy forms.'

'What?' Jake couldn't take it in. He felt like his dad was talking about someone else. 'Yunis, you mean?'

'I haven't accepted,' Dad said. 'That's

up to you. We can think about it. Talk to your mum.'

'They want *me*?' Jake said.

'*You*, Jake.'

Jake came to his senses. He looked over at the United manager. The Frenchman looked back at him like he was asking him a question.

'Tell him "Yes",' Jake said. 'Tell him "Yes!"'

New School

Jake thought he'd see more people he knew at the high school.

There were supposed to be about ten coming from his old primary school, but he hadn't spotted any of them yet. He hoped he'd see at least one familiar face soon, to calm his nerves.

There was a long path going up to the main building, between some playing fields. He walked through them, watching a group of older boys hoofing a football about. He hadn't realized the school grounds were so huge. And when he got to the school he realized that was huge too. He had to look at the map they'd sent to know where to go.

ENTRANCE 11

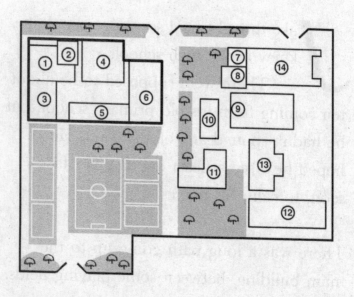

Jake didn't have a clue. He just wanted to turn round and go home.

He decided he would have to ask for some help. There were no teachers around, but there were two older students – a boy and a girl – standing at one of the entrances. And they looked like they were there to help the new year-sevens.

'You all right?' the boy said as Jake wandered up to him. The boy must have been at least fifteen.

Jake cleared his throat. 'Do you know where entrance eleven is? Please,' he said, his voice coming out all high-pitched.

The girl smiled at him.

'It's over there,' she said. 'The next one along. And don't worry. It's a nice school: just big. If you need any more help, just come and find us. I'm Shelley and this is David. We're in year eleven.'

Jake smiled and said thank you. Then he went along the building to find his classroom.

'Right, kids. Quieten down, please.'

The teacher at the front of the class was medium height with long brown hair. She was younger than most teachers. Jake liked her immediately: she had a friendly smile.

'My name is Miss Wing. I'd like to welcome you to the school. In this first lesson we're all going to get to know each other. I want you to talk to the person next to you. Find out about them. And then we'll all tell the rest of the class about our partners. OK?'

Miss Wing wrote a list of questions on the board for them to use to interview the person next to them.

Jake started asking his partner about himself.

He was called Euan.

He'd spent some of the summer holidays at his gran's, on the coast.

He liked sea fishing.

His favourite book was by Jeremy Strong. But he couldn't remember the title.

He supported United.

The two boys got talking about football. Jake told Euan he supported City. Euan winced: United fans weren't supposed to like City fans. So Jake told him about the trial.

That he was on United's books. He hadn't meant to. But he wanted Euan to like him.

'Right. Who wants to start?' Miss Wing said, ten minutes later, having brought the class back together.

Euan's hand shot up.

'This is Jake. He plays for United!'

And from then on Jake was OK.

He had friends.

He had people who wanted to sit next to him.

He was *the boy in 7F who's got schoolboy terms with United.*

Scruffy

The next few days were the best Jake had ever known.

He was happy. Really happy.

Every time he met someone and they asked how his football was going, he could spill the beans.

'I've got a place at United's Academy,' he'd say.

'What? *The* United?'

'Yeah.'

'How come you haven't told everybody?' they'd ask.

'I didn't want to sound like I was boasting,' Jake would say.

But every time he did tell someone about it, it gave him a thrill.

His grandma and grandad even threw him a party. Family members came from miles away to join in the celebrations. It was like having an extra birthday.

And the best bit was when Mum brought in a wrapped box – a present from the whole family: a pair of Nike T90 Laser football boots. The ones he'd wanted for ages.

But, when the day of the first training session at United arrived the following Monday, all Jake's euphoria had been replaced by nerves.

He came home from school as quickly as he could and got his bag together.

Boots.

Towel.

Tracksuit.

Kit.

The football kit United had given
him included a top with the United logo
on it. It felt strange having a United kit
in his bag. He'd not worn it yet. How
would he feel wearing a United badge? On
the one hand he was happy about it: he
was a United player, after all. On the
other hand he felt weird: he was still a
City fan.

Jake stuffed his City top in his bag. He
knew he could never wear it at the
Academy. He just wanted it with him for
luck.

He took off his school uniform and put
on his jeans and a T-shirt from the
weekend.

Then he came down the stairs, ready for his dad to drive him to the Academy.

'Back up the stairs, Jake,' Dad said. 'You're not wearing those clothes. Get something smart on. Your school uniform will do.'

'What?' Jake couldn't believe it.

'Something smart. You have to make a good impression.'

'I will. On the pitch,' Jake said, in a grumbling voice.

'And off it,' Dad said. 'Are you serious about this?'

'About what?'

'Playing for United. You know it's more than just about what you do on the pitch. It's about you representing the club. If you dress in scruffy clothes that's what they'll think of you as. Scruffy.'

Jake muttered something under his

breath and stamped back up the stairs to his bedroom.

Upstairs, he pulled his uniform back on. He hated being told what to do. He hated wearing his school uniform. He hated feeling so cross and anxious.

In the car, Jake said almost nothing. Dad asked him a couple of questions about school, but Jake gave one-word answers and stared out of the window. As the car drove through the streets, Jake watched people walking in parks and sitting talking in pub gardens. *They* all looked happy. But *he* wasn't happy. His stomach was tying itself in knots. And this was supposed to be the most exciting time of his life.

As they got nearer the Academy, Jake wanted more and more to talk to his dad.

He needed him to say nice things. To boost his confidence. Like he always did.

Turning right up the long drive, Dad must have sensed Jake's thoughts.

'I know you didn't want to wear the uniform,' Dad said. 'And I know you wanted to wear your jeans and trainers. But you need to make the right impression. The coaches will be looking at what sort of a person you are as well as what sort of a player.'

Jake shrugged. He knew his dad was right. He just didn't want to admit it.

'I'm nervous,' Jake said.

'I know. And I wouldn't want you to be any other way.'

Jake smiled. 'It's easy for you.'

'Listen,' Dad said, after a pause. 'This is your first day of being with a professional football club. You've worked for years to get here. But I want to ask you to do one thing for me.'

Jake frowned. 'What's that?'

'Enjoy it,' Dad said. 'You've earned that right. And you're as good a player as any there. Just enjoy it. Be yourself. And it'll go well.'

The Deadly Duo

The Academy looked brilliant.
Once they'd made it up the
drive and parked next to the old
stables, Jake had a chance to look at the
pitches again. They were the kind of lush
green you only see at the start of the
season, no stud marks and no muddy
patches.

The changing facilities looked nothing
like the ones at the teams he'd played for
before – usually either cramped rooms in

the backs of pubs, or council dressing
rooms, falling apart.

Jake was casting his eye over it all – and
the gathering group of boys and parents
outside the Academy entrance – when he
saw Yunis.

Yunis waved immediately and came over.

'How's it going?' asked Jake.

'Great,' Yunis said. He looked really
glad to see Jake. 'You got a place. That's
brilliant.'

'I know. I can't believe it,' Jake said. 'After you went, I saw that guy in the long coat again.'

'The first team manager?'

'Yeah, but I hadn't realized it was him. I must need glasses!'

'Did you talk to him?'

'No, but my dad did. Then they offered me the schoolboy contract. Like you.'

'We're gonna be great,' Yunis said. 'You and me. We'll be the Deadly Duo.'

Jake smiled, then pointed at the other boys. 'Are those the other under-twelves?'

'I don't know – I guess so.'

Then Jake remembered Yunis's dad. 'Is your dad here this time? Or your mum?'

'No. My dad wouldn't be seen dead here,' Yunis said, grinning. 'He hates it even more now I've got in.'

Jake laughed.

'Right, lads.' A loud voice cut all the conversations.

Jake recognized the voice immediately. It was the under-twelves team manager from the trial.

'As most of you know, my name is Steve Cooper. For the new lads, I'm one of the coaches who'll be working with you. We're joined by three new lads this season. Yunis over there . . .'

Yunis nodded at the others.

'Jake, standing next to Yunis. And Will, beside Chi.'

Jake raised his hand to wave to the other boys, and then looked over at Will. Will was the lad with the loud father from the trial.

As Steve Cooper talked, Jake looked around him. He could tell some of the other boys – ones who'd been here the year before – were checking him out. He had that uneasy feeling he always got when he was going to something for the first time, where he knew nobody and felt that everybody else knew each other. But he was also excited. Like Dad had said, this was his first day on the books of a professional football club. Even believing such a thing was hard. He was a *real* footballer.

'Right. Now we're all friends,' Steve said, 'let's get changed and on to the pitches. We'll go through some basic stuff for the season once we're all ready.'

Ryan

Jake walked out to the training fields with Yunis. Chi was just behind them.

They had to go over a bridge to reach the playing fields, above a swollen river running below. Then a huge area of grass opened up before them.

Jake and Yunis went over to talk to Will, who was tall and wiry.

'All right?' Jake said.

'Hello,' Will replied. 'I recognize you

from the trial. I *thought* you'd get in. Both of you.'

'I recognize you too,' Jake said, 'when you got selected.'

'You remember my dad, then?'

Jake smiled. 'Sort of. He was quite excited.'

'*Quite* excited?'

'It looked good to me,' Yunis said. 'He must have been proud of you.'

'He went over the top a bit,' Will said.

'It's his life's fantasy to get me playing for United. He won't be happy until I've lifted the Champions League trophy. As captain.'

Jake smiled at Yunis, who shrugged.

Yunis turned round and waited for Chi to catch up. 'Are you new too?' Yunis said.

'No, I was here last year. And the year before.'

'What's it like?'

'It's great,' Chi said.

'Who's the captain?' Will asked, joining in.

'Ryan,' Chi said. 'He's the tall one with jet-black hair beside Ben, who's the lad with his socks down. Ryan's been at United since he was eight. They reckon he's the next John Terry. He's a great player, but –' Chi paused – 'keep on his good side.'

Jake looked ahead at Ryan, who was carrying a huge net bag full of footballs.

As Jake watched him, Ryan stared back. Jake wasn't sure he liked the way Ryan had looked at him.

'The other tall lad, just ahead of them,' Chi went on, 'is Tomasz. He's the keeper. He joined last season. He's Polish and lives with his dad. They moved to the UK last year. He's really good, but he can have his off-days.'

Jake tried to remember the names that Chi had told him. Ryan, Ben, Tomasz.

He liked Chi. He was friendly. And – Jake was pleased to see – Chi was about the same height as he was. *Not* too small for football.

When they reached the first playing field, Steve stopped them. Jake looked at the other pitches. Two other teams were training already. A group of older kids and some eight- or nine-year-olds. Jake could hear the voices of the coaches above the noise of the players.

'Right, lads. Each of you take a ball and let's have five minutes of keepy-uppies. To warm yourselves up.'

Ryan began to kick balls to each player, taking them out of the bag he'd carried. Jake was last to get a ball and Ryan sent it flying over his head into some trees.

Jake assumed it was an accident and laughed along when he heard Ryan and Ben laughing too – until he saw Chi frowning.

City Shirt

By the time Jake and Chi got back to the dressing rooms after the first training session, half of the players had already gone. Jake had stayed back on the pitch to help Steve put the balls back into the net bag. He thought that would be a good thing to do. Like his dad had said: be helpful. But it meant he missed out on talking to some of the other players.

Pulling his boots off, he was surprised to see Ryan standing over a bag, holding a

City shirt. For a minute he thought Ryan was a City fan too. That it could be a good way of making friends with him.

Until Jake realized it was *his* City shirt. And that Ryan had taken it out of *his* bag.

'What's this?' Ryan said, looking straight at Jake and Chi, grinning. Ben and two of the other players were standing behind Ryan.

'A City shirt,' Jake said, feeling small next to Ryan, who was much taller than him. But he wasn't going to stand down: it was his City shirt; and, even though he was a United player, he was still a City fan. And proud of it.

'This is United, Jakey. Not City. I think you've come to the wrong club.'

Jake didn't know what to say. He didn't want to cause trouble on his first day, so he just shrugged. Even though Ryan had called him Jakey. A name he hated to be called.

Ryan stared at Jake for a few seconds, then threw the shirt down on the floor. Ben and the other lads laughed. Jake picked up the shirt and carried on getting changed.

'Ben. Do you think we should have City players in our dressing rooms?' Ryan said.

'No,' Ben said.

'Do you think we need to keep an eye on Jakey-boy?'

'Yeah.'

'We'll have to watch him, won't we? Make sure he's really committed to United. Maybe he's a spy.'

'Yeah,' Ben said.

Jake wondered if Ben knew any other words than 'No' and 'Yeah'. But he kept his head down, until Ryan and Ben left the room, still laughing.

'See you on Wednesday training, Jakey-boy,' Ryan jeered as he let the dressing-room door swing shut.

Jake couldn't work out why Ryan was being so horrible.

'Don't worry about Ryan,' Chi said, after a pause. 'He's OK really.'

Jake and Chi were the only ones left in the dressing rooms.

'What's up with him, then?' Jake said. 'Was it really that he didn't like my shirt?'

'A bit,' Chi said.

'Is there something else?' Jake said.

'Sort of . . .'

'What? I don't understand.'

'The main thing –' Chi paused – 'is that you're a left winger. And last year's left winger was Aaron, Ryan's best mate. Aaron was released at the end of last season and Ryan's upset that you've taken his place.

He'll forget about it soon – just ignore him.'

'It'll be hard.'

'I know. But if you think Ryan's hard on you, you should see his mum. She's so hard on Ryan, you wouldn't believe it. She's a nutter.'

Tomasz

It was Saturday – and Jake felt weird.
Saturday morning meant four
Weetabix with a chopped banana, then
meeting up with the others at the village
hall, either to play at home or travel to an
away game in a fleet of cars.

But not today.

Today he was lying on the sofa, watching
Soccer AM. But he felt so funny about there
being no game, he couldn't concentrate.

Dad was in the kitchen.

Jake switched the TV off and stared at the wall.

Dad came in immediately. 'What's up?'

'Nothing.'

'Are you bored?'

'I am,' Jake admitted. 'That's going to be the hardest bit: I wish I could play for the village too.'

'Well, you can't,' Dad said. 'That's the rule. So why don't we do something?'

'Like what?' Jake said. He was hoping that his dad was thinking the same thing as he was: going to watch City at home.

'What's the one thing you never get to do, because you had to play on a Saturday afternoon?'

Jake grinned, hiding his face. 'Dunno?'

'City,' Dad said.

Jake swivelled round. 'Can we? Please? Can we?'

'Come on. We'll get down there early.
It's a midday kick-off.'

Jake was up the stairs before Dad had
finished talking.

The City stadium was busy: long queues for
burger vans and at the club shop; TV
broadcast units parked up in one of the main
car parks – a huge satellite dish facing the sky.

Once Dad had got the tickets they had
to walk around the stadium three times.

Dad always did this. Clockwise. For luck. They had to fight their way past huge crowds coming the other way.

Halfway round they met Tomasz and his dad.

Tomasz caught Jake's eye and smiled.

'I don't believe it,' Jake said. 'Are you a City fan?'

'I am. My dad is too. That's why we moved here, rather than London. He wanted to be able to watch City.'

'Does Ryan know?'

Tomasz screwed his face up. 'He gave you trouble, didn't he?'

'He found my City shirt.'

'Oh dear,' Tomasz said. 'He's not found mine yet.'

Jake and Tomasz laughed. Jake noticed his dad deep in conversation with Tomasz's dad.

'Is Ryan going to be all right?' Jake asked Tomasz. 'You've been at United for half a season, haven't you?'

'Since last year,' Tomasz said. 'Ryan's never happy. Always looking to have a go at someone. He takes after his mum.'

'Is she really bad? Chi mentioned her.'

'*Really* bad. And the worse she is, the worse he gets.'

'What do you mean?'

'I mean if she's on his back, he'll be on someone else's back. Taking it out on them.'

'Great,' Jake said.

'But you get to like him. If someone fouls you from another team he'll be right there for you.'

Jake smiled. That was good, at least.

He heard the first songs coming from the main City end of the ground.

'What stand are you in?' Tomasz said.

'The other end. We only got tickets today.'

The two dads were shaking hands.

Jake and Tomasz smiled at each other.

'See you on Monday night,' Jake said.

'Yeah, see you,' Tomasz said. 'And don't tell Ryan about me and City. He's already on my case because I don't support England!'

Fame

Training with United was going well.
And school was going well.

In fact, school was *great*.

Jake had been told over and over that starting high school could be hard. That the school would be bigger – and so would the other students. And it *was* bigger. And the students *were* bigger. But now that word got around that he was a United player, Jake was a minor celebrity.

Half the school seemed to know his

name, saying hello to him in the corridors. Older boys would ask him which United first-team players he knew. Even some of the teachers treated him like he was different.

One morning, four year-nines approached him. Two girls and two boys.

'Are you Jake Oldfield?' one of the girls said.

'Yeah.'

Jake was wary. Girls – especially older girls – starting a conversation with you was usually trouble. They were taller than him – both with long straight hair. One of them was wearing eye make-up. The boys had short hair; one was much taller than the other.

'Are you a United player, then?' the taller lad asked.

'Yeah.'

'Can you only say "Yeah"?' The girl again.

'No,' Jake said.

Both the girls laughed. Then one of them said, 'You're funny.'

Jake shrugged. He didn't know what to say, let alone how to be funny.

The one thing he had to admit about the high school was that he found talking to older students hard. It had been easier at his old school, at the end, when *he* was one of the oldest.

'So, are you rich?' the girl without make-up said.

'No.'

'David Luxton in year eight says you got a hundred thousand pounds when you signed for United,' the taller lad said.

Jake tried not to smile.

It wasn't the first time he'd heard this. In the beginning he'd denied it. But, as the rumour wasn't going to go away, he'd got tired of it and decided to let them wonder.

'I'm not allowed to say,' Jake said.

'So you're dead rich, then?' the girl with make-up said.

Jake shrugged.

It felt weird talking to year-nines like this.

'Do you know Alec Hodkinson?' the shorter boy said.

Alec Hodkinson was a young United player, who also played for England's under-twenty-ones.

Jake wanted to say yes. To make out he and Alec Hodkinson were best mates. But something told him not to.

'I've never even seen him,' Jake said. 'And . . . if you must know, I didn't get paid by United. They're not allowed to pay me until I'm sixteen.'

Both girls rolled their eyes and started to walk away.

'Have you got a sponsorship deal?' the taller boy asked.

Jake wasn't even sure what a sponsorship deal was. He shook his head and went off to maths.

United or City?

*I*t was the fourth training session of the season. Jake knew all the other players now and felt like he was one of the team.

He'd been a bit self-conscious coming into a squad where twelve of the fifteen boys had played together the season before. And he was particularly uneasy around Ryan. But it was OK now – especially as he had made such a good friend in Yunis.

Today, unusually, Jake was the last to get

changed. He had been a bit late, his dad's car getting caught up in traffic coming across town. Everyone else was out on the pitches by the time he arrived. Jake was rushing, stuffing his clothes into his bag and searching for his shin pads.

Suddenly, he heard the sound of studs coming across the concrete outside the dressing rooms. Ryan came in, a little breathless, but grinning.

'We're having a proper match today,' Ryan said.

'Great,' Jake said, as happy that Ryan was talking to him as he was that they were playing a game and not just doing drills.

Ryan had his United top on. He pointed at Jake's top.

'Half of us are in United tops for the game, half in City. Have you got your City top with you? Steve told me to ask you to wear it.'

Jake grinned. 'Yes,' he said.

He pulled his City shirt out of his bag.

Ryan nodded and went back outside. 'See you out there. Steve says we're starting in two minutes. I'll tell him you'll be there in a second.'

'Thanks,' Jake said, lacing up his boots. He felt good about his chat with Ryan. Ryan had actually been *nice*.

It was strange putting his City shirt on after wearing a United one for the last two weeks. Strange, but good. He was a City fan, after all, whoever he played for.

Once he was changed, Jake sprinted outside, running head down, so he could get on the pitches in time for Steve to start things off.

It was only when he was in the middle of

the pitch that he noticed half the players were wearing United tops – and that the other half were wearing orange vests over their United shirts. No one was wearing a *City* top.

Except Jake.

Ryan had tricked him. And everyone was looking at Jake.

At first he heard a single boo. Just one voice. Then another joined in. And another. And suddenly half of the lads were booing.

Jake didn't know what to do. If he'd been at school – or playing with mates – he'd have risen to it, shown that he wore his City shirt with pride. But here it was different. He didn't know if he had to show loyalty to United. Or if he could still show he was proud to be a City fan.

Then he heard Steve's voice, loud and hard.

'OLDFIELD!'

Jake turned to face Steve, but said nothing.

'What is *that*?'

'What?'

'That *shirt* you're wearing?'

'It's my . . . er . . . my . . . City shirt . . .'
He was about to say that Ryan had told him to wear it, but thought better of it. If he brought Ryan in as an excuse, it would only cause more trouble.

'Take it off,' Steve said.

Jake took off the shirt.

Ryan grabbed it off him before Jake could do anything. 'Shall I put it in the bin, Steve?'

'Give it back to Jake,' Steve said in an even voice, quieter now.

Jake took the shirt back off Ryan, ignoring the sneer from his team captain.

'Take it to the side of the pitch, then put one of these vests on.'

Steve threw Jake a luminous orange vest. Then he went on as if nothing had happened.

'Right, lads. Attack against defence. You lot in United tops are defending. The rest of you – Jake too, OK? – attacking. We've got our first game on Sunday. Blackburn Rovers away. We've worked a lot on technique. But now's the time to put all that into practice.'

Blackburn Rovers
v United

Jake's first match for United was not
going well.

He'd fantasized the night before
about his debut, while trying to get to sleep:
beating defenders time and time again,
sliding balls in to Yunis and an avalanche
of goals that would be remembered when
he was a regular first-teamer in ten years'
time.

But that was the last thing that was
happening. Blackburn Rovers were all over

United. Their two strikers were running rings round the United defence. And their defenders were like a brick wall for United's attackers.

By half-time it was two–nil to Rovers and Jake had hardly seen the ball.

Ryan – who always brought it out from the back – was only playing it to Ben on the right. He hadn't even looked at Jake.

*

Early in the second half United let a third goal in. The two quick Rovers strikers were two-against-two on United's central defenders, James and Ryan. James tried to tackle one of the players, but was too slow. Ryan was tracking the second, but, as he took the ball, the striker shoulder-charged Ryan off the ball, then slammed the ball past Tomasz.

Three–nil. Disaster.

But it was a fair tackle, Jake thought. *Shoulder-charges are legal.* He knew that after he'd been shoulder-charged during the trials. And he could tell Steve agreed with the referee not to give a foul. Steve was nodding.

But Ryan's mum *didn't* agree.

Jake had heard about Ryan's mum. But he was still surprised by what she did next.

'That was a foul. A foul!' she screamed, running on to the side of the pitch. 'Don't you know the rules, referee?'

The referee stared at her for a moment and glanced at Steve.

Then things got worse. Ushered away from the pitch by another parent, Ryan's mum suddenly escaped and ran back to the sidelines. 'No goal! No goal! Our Ryan was *fouled*!'

The referee was shocked now. He'd probably never seen anything like this before. He looked over at Steve again and spoke. Jake was standing near the referee so he heard what was said.

'Get that woman off the pitch *now* – or I'll abandon this game and report you to the authorities.'

Jake watched as Steve went over to Ryan's mum, took her firmly by the arm and led her off the pitch, all the time talking to her in a quiet, but firm, voice.

Then Jake looked at Ryan. He was

staring at the ground, his face red. Somehow he looked smaller and less of the bully that Jake had taken him for. He looked younger too.

Jake felt like going over and asking if Ryan was OK. But he knew he'd better not. He didn't think Ryan would like sympathy.

Jake looked for his dad, but couldn't see him. He'd probably gone off to the toilet.

The referee restarted the game. Three–nil. And it wasn't long before it was four.

Down the Left

Towards the end of the game, the ball came to Jake's feet. Not from Ryan, but from James, the other central defender, who'd started to play a more dominant role, leaving Ryan further back in defence.

Jake took the ball past a defender with his first touch – and ran into the space ahead of him. He put on a burst of power, just beating the defender.

Then he was away, dribbling at speed. At last: a chance to prove himself.

As a second defender came across to cover him, Jake looked up and saw Chi on his right. He tapped the ball to Chi, who played it to the other side of the defender. Jake was on to it. A perfect one-two. He looked up. Yunis was on the near post, with Ben on the far post.

Jake played it low and hard to Yunis.

Yunis intercepted the ball, turned and slotted it home.

Goal!

The first of the season.

But no one cheered.

Yunis did jog over to shake Jake's hand. But that was it.

There wasn't much to celebrate.

Blackburn Rovers 4 United 1.

*

'You looked like you'd never met, let alone trained together before,' Steve said. He wasn't shouting. He was calm, looking each boy in the eye. He hadn't mentioned Ryan's mum. And Jake didn't expect him to. Parents were talked to in Steve's office.

'We were OK apart from Tomasz,' Ryan shouted, eyeing the team's keeper. Ryan looked pink-faced, still angry or embarrassed. Jake couldn't tell which.

'Don't blame it all on Tomasz,' Steve said. 'He was exposed by the defence. And by the midfield. It could have been a lot worse without him.'

Tomasz looked down at the floor. He looked sad, his tall, wiry body hunched over. Jake tried to catch his eye, to give him some support. But Tomasz didn't look up.

'We need to vary it,' Steve said.

'Everything went down the right to Ben. Hardly anything went down the left.'

Jake didn't look at Ryan, but he was glad to hear this from Steve.

'It's a team game, Ryan,' Steve said. 'I want to see Jake getting more of the ball. Jake and Yunis have a good understanding. Let's bring them into it more next week.'

'OK, Steve,' Ryan said, staring at the door.

'So let's use this as a learning experience,' Steve said, finishing off. 'We've found some things out about ourselves this week. Next week we'll do better. OK?'

Ryan, Ben, Tomasz and Jake were the last to leave the dressing rooms.

Jake expected some stick from Ryan, after the criticism Ryan had had from Steve. But all the stick was going Tomasz's way.

'What was it with you today, Tomasz?'
Ryan said.

'It was hard,' Tomasz said slowly. 'I was
. . . exposed.'

'You're only saying "exposed" because
Steve said it,' Ryan said. 'I bet you don't
even know what "exposed" means.'

'I do.'

'Go on then?'

'It means *alone*,' Tomasz said, standing
up.

Jake half-stood, then sat down when Ryan stared at him.

'No, it doesn't,' Ben said. 'It means there were no defenders in front of you. And there *were*. Four!'

Tomasz shrugged and walked out of the room.

Jake wanted to go after him. He wished he'd stuck up for his new friend.

'My mum says his dad shouldn't even be over here,' Ryan said in an angry voice. 'All the Poles. Taking our jobs.'

'That's right,' Ben said.

Jake kept his eyes on his kitbag.

'Don't you reckon?' Ryan said. 'Jake?'

'What?'

'That Tomasz shouldn't even be in the team. He's rubbish. And he's *Polish*.'

Jake shrugged, then nodded reluctantly.

He immediately felt bad.

Sunday 25 September
Blackburn Rovers 4 United 1
Goals: Yunis
Bookings: Connor, James

Under-twelves manager's marks out of ten for each player:

Tomasz	5
Connor	5
James	6
Ryan	6
Ronan	6
Chi	6
Sam	5
Will	6
Jake	6
Yunis	7
Ben	6

Aaron

'*T*hat was a good move at the end. With Yunis,' Jake's dad said.

They were driving home from Rovers.

Jake said nothing back to his dad. He didn't feel like talking. He hadn't even told him about Ryan's mum, knowing his dad had been away at the time.

'So how do you feel after your first game?'

'We got stuffed, Dad.'

'But *you* did OK, when that defender actually passed it to you.'

'But he didn't, did he?'

Dad paused. 'Why's that?'

'Dunno.'

Dad paused again. Then said, 'You seem to get on well with that striker. What's he like?'

'He's great. He was at the trial. Do you remember?'

'Yes. Fast lad,' Dad said. 'So is he a mate?'

'Sort of, I suppose,' Jake said. 'His dad never comes to watch him.'

Dad nodded. 'What about the others?'

'I don't know them that well yet.'

'Tomasz. The lad we met at City. Is he OK?'

Jake felt a shudder of shame go through him. 'I didn't really speak to him today. He left straight after the match.'

'I saw him,' Dad said.

'Was he OK?' Jake said. Too quickly.

'Tomasz? Maybe not. He looked a bit cross coming out of the dressing rooms. I was talking to his dad. I assumed it was because he'd let four in.'

'There's this lad . . .' Jake started to say.

'Yeah?'

Jake paused. He wanted to tell Dad about Ryan. But how?

'One of the lads was picking on Tomasz,' Jake said. 'Saying stuff.'

'What sort of stuff?'

'You know.'

'I don't,' Dad said. 'I wasn't there.'

'Nothing,' Jake said.

'Come on, Jake . . .'

'That he didn't belong here. Because he's Polish.'

Dad frowned, but said nothing.

'It's nothing,' Jake said, worried his dad would raise it with Steve. 'The team didn't do well. It's the first time we've all played together. It's just that.'

'What's that defender called?'

'Which one?' Jake was shocked his dad had hit on Ryan straight away.

'You know which one I mean.'

Jake said nothing for a moment. Then he confessed. 'Ryan.'

'Is it him?' Dad waited for Jake to speak.

'Yes,' Jake said.

'And is he giving you trouble too?'

Jake kept quiet for a minute. Then another minute. Then he had to speak.

'Last year, Ryan's best mate was on the left wing. Aaron. But he was released at the end of the season. Chi told me. And that's why Ryan doesn't like me. He reckons if he makes me look rubbish he can get his mate back in the team. But you mustn't say anything,' he added. 'About me or Tomasz.'

Dad spent a few seconds watching the road. 'You don't want me to talk to Steve?' he said.

Jake sat forward quickly. 'No, I don't.'

'OK,' Dad said. 'But if it happens again, will you tell me? I won't do anything if you do. I just want to know.'

Neither Jake nor Dad spoke for the rest of the journey back. Jake's dream had been to return jubilantly home. To tell Mum the news of a great win – and his part in it.

Instead he just felt depressed.

But not as depressed as he would have

been travelling home alone, Jake thought. Like Yunis.

Jake gazed out of the window. Then he turned to his dad.

'Thanks for bringing me, Dad,' he said. 'For coming to training every week.'

'That's OK.'

'Dad?'

'Yes.'

'You know Tomasz's dad?'

'Yes. What about him?'

'What does he do? As a job?'

'He's a doctor at the hospital. A really good one: he's always in the newspaper. Why?'

'Nothing,' Jake said. 'Just asking.'

United v Middlesbrough

The second game was a bit better than the first.

United were playing much deeper than the week before. Steve had worked with them, teaching the midfielders to protect the defenders, so they weren't left so exposed. And it was working.

But Jake still felt like he was out of it for long periods of time. And when he did go for the ball, he always seemed to be

offside. He would move forward to attack
– and the linesman's flag would go up.
Every time. It was so frustrating. He
couldn't remember *ever* getting caught
offside before, but the other team were
more interested in stopping United with
offsides than by actually playing football
themselves.

But at least Jake didn't have his dad on
his case. Ryan's mum was back: shouting at
Ryan this time, not the referee.

'Ryan . . . get your finger out . . . cover
your man . . . what's the matter with you?'

Ryan was getting more and more angry
on the pitch, rushing into tackles, hoofing
the ball up field instead of short-passing it
along the ground like Steve had taught
them.

Then Jake heard Steve calling to *him*.
'Play behind the last man, Jake.'

So Jake tried to stay onside.

But seconds later, Ryan would say it too. 'Play behind the last man.'

And Jake was trying. But now, every time the ball came near him, the last Middlesbrough defender would get it, because he was further up the pitch.

This is stupid, Jake thought. Whatever he chose to do seemed to be the wrong thing. He felt like he was tied up in knots.

He was almost relieved when the final whistle went.

But relief was the last thing he felt a few minutes later.

'That was poor, lads,' Steve said. His voice was a little harder than it had been after the first game.

United had lost two–one.

'Let's go through the game player by player. Let's try and sort this out.'

Steve talked about each player, starting with Tomasz in goal, through the defence. He spent a lot of time talking about Ryan. How he needed to pass to Jake more. Use the left wing as well as the right.

Eventually he came to Jake.

'And Jake. We need to work on the offside, don't we?'

'I'm sorry, Steve,' Jake said. 'I just couldn't get on the right side of him.'

'Well, it's something we have to work on. You've got such pace, but you need to time your runs. You did it during your trial – timed it brilliantly. Let's have a chat tomorrow. Is your dad coming in?'

Jake nodded.

'Right, we'll talk about it more then.'

Jake felt like he'd fallen off the side of the world. What did Steve want his dad for? Surely this was about training? Nothing to do with his dad.

But a question came into his mind. He couldn't help it: was Steve going to release him?

The players gathered their bags after Steve had finished talking. Ryan and Ben came over to Jake, catching him on his own. Jake

could tell they were going to be nasty to
him. Just by their faces.

'Are you Polish too, or something?' Ryan
said.

Ben sniggered.

Jake said nothing.

He was aware Tomasz was right
behind him, listening. He didn't want Ryan
to say something about Polish people that
would make him have to agree with him

again. He still wished he'd stuck up for Tomasz when Ryan had been horrible before.

'You played like *you* don't understand English,' Ryan said. 'Offside. How many times do you need to hear it said to understand it?'

Jake still said nothing. He just stared back at Ryan, then Ben. He wanted them to know he didn't think they were funny, that he didn't agree with them. At all.

Ten minutes later Jake left the dressing rooms. Ryan was outside; on his mobile, grinning.

'Aaron,' he said into the phone.

Jake couldn't help but listen.

'I've got some good news for you,' Ryan went on. 'Just a minute . . . someone's listening.' Ryan stared at Jake and grinned again, then disappeared round the back of the dressing rooms.

And Jake felt even more sure he was about to be dropped from the team.

Sunday 2 October
United 1 Middlesbrough 2
Goals: Yunis
Bookings: Connor, James

Under-twelves manager's marks out of ten for each player:

Tomasz	6
Connor	6
James	7
Ryan	5
Ronan	6
Chi	7
Sam	6
Will	6
Jake	5
Yunis	7
Ben	6

Yunis's Dad

'You all right, Jake?'

Jake was walking through the car park when Yunis came up behind him. Jake's dad had had to leave quickly after the game, so, unusually, Jake had to make his own way home.

'No,' Jake said. 'I was rubbish today. I can't get into it.' Jake wondered if he should tell Yunis about his fears of being dropped.

'We were *all* rubbish,' Yunis said.

'*You* weren't. You scored. And you weren't

offside even once. I was – ten times at least.'

'It's not just you. It's Ryan. If he's not going to pass it to you, how can you expect to be ready and onside?'

'I should be,' Jake said. 'That's all.'

'Is there anything else?' Yunis asked, after a pause.

'Like what?'

'What Chi told you about Ryan's mate. The winger. Aaron.'

Jake couldn't believe Yunis had said what he'd said. It was like he was reading his mind. He didn't really want to talk about it. But there was no point in denying it now.

He blurted it out. 'Do you reckon Steve *will* drop me? And let Aaron back in?'

'He can't,' Yunis said, surprised.

'Why not?' Jake said. 'He wants a winning team. If I'm worse than this Aaron, he *should* drop me and bring him back in.'

A horn beeped behind them.

Jake looked round, expecting to see his dad waiting for him after all. He would have liked that. Talking it through with Dad.

But, instead, a tall Asian man in a suit leaned out of a silver Mercedes.

Yunis's face lit up. 'It's my dad!'

He jogged over to his dad's car,

gesturing for Jake to join him. He was grinning, like he was really excited.

'This is Jake,' Yunis said. 'Jake, this is my dad.'

Yunis's dad shook Jake's hand. 'Hello, young man. Can I drop you somewhere? I've come to take Yunis home.'

'Are you going through the centre of town?' Jake said.

'Certainly. Jump in.'

Jake got in. Yunis's dad seemed OK. He'd expected an ogre from what Yunis had said about him.

Yunis got in the back of the car after Jake. 'Did you see the game, Dad?'

'No, Yunis. I was here in the car park.'

'You should have come to see the last few minutes. I scored.' Yunis's voice had lost its excitement.

'I came to pick you up. Not watch your

footballing,' his dad said. 'Get you home
sooner, so you can catch up on your studies.
You're losing whole days playing this
football game.'

Yunis's face dropped, then he looked at
Jake. Jake smiled, trying to be supportive.
But Yunis looked down to play with the
strap of his bag.

They drove on in silence, Jake not
daring to speak and wishing he'd caught the
bus instead.

The Phone Call

Monday evening. Training night. Jake had had a bad day at school. He hadn't been able to concentrate at all because he was worrying about the football.

Dad was back from work early, as usual, so he could run Jake to the Academy.

'Right, Jake,' he said. 'Let's go.' Dad was already putting his jacket on.

'It's not on,' Jake said.

'Not on?' Dad stopped, one arm of his jacket hanging limp at his side.

'Steve called it off,' Jake said. 'He's just phoned. Something about the first team needing the pitches.'

'Oh right.' Dad paused for a moment, then smiled. 'Let's watch the match on telly tonight, then, eh?'

Upstairs, Jake switched on his PlayStation. He'd play *Football Manager* until the match started. To take his mind off what was happening at United. It wasn't true about training being off. It *was* still on. It'd be starting in less than an hour. Jake just couldn't face it.

Sitting there, he felt guilty. Guilty about missing training. Guilty about lying to his dad. Guilty about letting Steve down. But he didn't want to face Steve. To be told he was going to be released.

And he definitely didn't want to see Ryan.

How could he go to the Academy – where he'd wanted to go for as long as he could remember – then be asked to leave?

He'd rather never go back.

It was half-time in the match on TV – City versus Argyle. City were two–nil up. Dad hadn't mentioned training and Jake was enjoying just sitting with him.

Then the phone rang.

Even before Dad picked it up, Jake knew it was Steve.

He jumped up off his seat. 'I'm going to bed,' he said.

Mum and Dad looked at him, both frowning. Why was he going to bed, with City winning two–nil?

Closing the front-room door, Jake listened to his dad on the phone.

'Hello?'

A pause.

'Hello, Steve.'

It *was* Steve.

'Jake? No, he's here.' Another long pause: Dad was listening. 'I see . . .'

Then Jake was on his way up the stairs, straight into his room, light out, curtains closed, under the duvet.

It was just a matter of time before Dad came up the stairs. And, when he did, he was going to be furious.

Dad

Half an hour later there was a
gentle knock on the door. Jake had
been staring at the ceiling. Waiting.
The door pushed open. Dad.

'Can I come in?'

Jake's plan, to pretend to be asleep,
seemed stupid now.

'Yeah,' Jake said.

He flicked on his City table lamp.

Dad sat on the end of Jake's bed. 'That
was Steve,' he said.

'I know.'

'He was just back from training. He wanted to know if you were OK.'

Jake looked away, but said nothing.

'What's going on?' Dad said.

Jake had expected Dad to be cross. To feel that Jake had let him down. But he was being OK. Like he always was. So Jake decided to be honest. After lying to Dad before, he owed him that.

'I think they're going to bring Aaron back. The lad who used to play on the left last season. They're going to release me.'

'Has Steve said that?'

Jake paused, surprised because Dad sounded angry at Steve, not at him.

'No,' Jake said.

Dad sighed. 'Who said it, then?'

Jake tried to think. Ryan had said it – sort of. And Steve had said he wanted to talk to Dad. Then he'd overheard Ryan talking to Aaron on the phone.

But had anyone actually said it?

'I dunno,' Jake said.

'These games,' Dad said. 'The first two. They've not gone well, have they?'

'No.'

'And you think they're going to release you?'

'They *are*.'

'Why do you think that?'

'Steve . . .'

'What about him?'

'He wants to talk to me – and *you*. What else could that mean?'

Dad stood up. 'Wait here,' he said.

Dad left Jake alone. Jake heard him run down the stairs, then ask Mum a question, and finally come back up the stairs. He had a cardboard folder in his hand. He took out a piece of paper.

'What's this?' Dad asked.

'My contract,' Jake said.

'What does it say here?' Dad pointed at a line of the text.

'That I'm signed to play for twelve months. Until August.'

'Right.'

'But if I'm rubbish . . .'

'Jake. You've played two games. You're not rubbish. If you're out of form, Steve might put you on the bench. But so far he hasn't, has he? Don't you remember what they said when you signed on? That they thought you had great potential? That they wanted to work with you for a year? At *least* a year. So that they could develop you as a player?'

Jake shrugged.

'Have you forgotten what a good player you are?' Dad said.

'Maybe I'm not a good player.'

Dad pulled the bedclothes off Jake.

'Come on.'

'What?'

'The fields. Now.'

'It's dark.'

'There's enough light coming from the street lamps. Nothing serious. Just shots in. Come on.'

Playing with Dad

On Wednesday after school, Dad and Jake were driving across the city again. Towards the United Academy.

Jake felt nervous. Before training today they had the appointment – with Steve. Jake was glad that Dad was coming now. The club said it always had to be like that. If a player was having trouble – or if there was something important to talk about – a parent had to come too.

For the last two nights Jake had been
out on the fields with his dad. Practising like
they used to. Wearing his City top. Jake
hadn't thought about it, but since he'd
signed for United, he'd stopped playing with
his dad completely.

As they had kicked the ball to each
other, Jake remembered how much he
enjoyed playing football, whether he was
playing for United or just playing with his
dad.

And Dad had convinced him that Steve
wasn't going to replace him. It was just
going to be a chat about how to make
things work better for Jake.

'Are you OK, then?' Dad asked, slowing
down in some heavy traffic.

'Yes thanks.'

'Remember what I said yesterday . . .'

'Dad?'

Jake wanted to interrupt. He knew Dad was going to say things to make him feel confident. But Jake had something to say too.

'. . . that you just have to play your own game,' Dad went on. 'And focus. You're fast. You can control the –'

'Dad?'

Dad stopped talking and looked at Jake. 'What?'

'Did *you* miss us playing on the fields?'

Dad smiled. 'I did miss it, yes.' He was quiet for a few seconds, then said, 'But I've not been lazing about. I've been coming to see you at the Academy, haven't I?'

'I know. But it's not like playing, is it?' Jake said.

'No. And the last two nights have been fun. But I'd rather see you at the Academy.'

'Yeah?'

'Yes. Every time I see you training or playing, it makes me feel so proud. Every time I see you touch the ball . . .'

'So that's better than playing with me?'

'On the whole, yes,' Dad said.

Jake felt good. *Every time I get the ball,* he thought, *I'm going to play for Dad. I'm going to make him even prouder.*

'Except,' Dad said, interrupting Jake's thoughts. 'If you ever fancy a kick about . . . you know where I live.'

Jake grinned.

The Appointment

'Come in, Jake,' Steve said. 'Mr Oldfield.'

Steve shook Jake's dad's hand and closed the door behind them.

Jake felt like he was at the doctor's or the dentist's. Like something bad was going to happen to him.

The office was small and stacked with cones and a large bag of footballs. Two shelves were packed with coaching manuals and box files. Jake was surprised it was such a mess.

'OK,' Steve said. 'You've been with us four weeks now. I just wanted to see how everything was for you. Both of you. I always do this. Make sure there are no teething problems.'

Jake felt a wave of relief. So this was normal. Just a chat to make sure everything was OK. He felt Dad's hand on his back.

'Jake?' Steve said. 'Anything to report? Any worries?'

'No,' Jake said. 'Everything's fine.'

'You sure? We can be open here. Whatever we say stays in this room. It's a private chat. It's as important to me how you develop off the pitch, as on it.'

'No. It's fine.'

'OK then,' Steve said. 'Mr Oldfield? Are you happy? Anything you'd like to say?'

Dad stared at Jake and raised an
eyebrow.

Jake knew Dad wouldn't say anything.
Or push him to say anything. It was down
to him.

There was a long pause. Jake realized
that Steve was waiting for him to speak.
He stared at the bag of balls. He longed

to be out on the fields playing. With Dad. Just playing football without any complications.

Then it just came out.

'I'm worried you might release me and bring back that lad . . . Aaron. And I'm worried that you think you've made a mistake . . . that you'd like him back . . . that he fitted in better. And that at the trial you thought I was good, but that I'm not. That all the other players are up to it and I'm not . . .'

Steve smiled. 'Sorry,' he said, quickly. 'I didn't mean to smile.'

He stood up and breathed in. 'Jake. There is *no* chance of that happening. You are signed for a year. The club is committed to you for that year. And for more years after that, I hope sincerely. When you signed that contract, I did too. It's my job to bring out your talent – and you have that in abundance. We want to give you the best chance of becoming a professional footballer. It won't always be easy. But that's why we brought you here: because we think you can do it.'

Jake smiled, looking at Dad. 'I know,' he said to Steve. 'I'm sorry. I knew that.'

'I understand you feel like this, Jake. It's normal. It's a big thing, being here. Starting this stage of your footballing career. And if you have any doubts like that again, come to me and we'll talk them through.'

Steve sat down and leaned back in his chair.

'I don't know where you got your ideas about Aaron from,' he said, raising an eyebrow. 'Is everything else OK? You getting on all right with the other lads?'

Jake felt like being honest. As honest as he could be.

'It's quite difficult sometimes,' he said. 'Finding my place. I get on with Yunis and Chi. And Will. But one or two of the others are harder to deal with than the rest.'

Steve nodded.

Jake didn't want to say any more. He didn't want to name any names.

'I understand, Jake,' Steve said. 'But if you have any more trouble, come to me. And, by the way, not that this is anything you've said to me today, but one thing we don't accept at this club is bullying. If it happens, I stamp it out. I make sure all the lads know that. OK?'

'OK,' Jake said.

Steve stood up.

'In a month's time, Jake, you're going

to be a key part of this team. I want you here for the long run. Not just for two games.'

Jake smiled. He felt better.

Attack and Defence

Jake was sitting laughing with Yunis in the dressing rooms. But then Ryan came over – and suddenly Jake felt cold all over.

Ryan was grinning.

'I saw Aaron at school today,' Ryan said. 'He says United have been in touch.'

Jake said nothing for a moment. But he was determined that he wasn't going to let this happen any more. He was going to take control.

'No, he didn't,' Jake said calmly, looking Ryan square in the face.

'How can you be sure of that?' Ryan said, smirking.

'I know, that's all.' Jake kept his eyes on Ryan, until Ryan looked away.

'We'll see,' Ryan said, turning and walking towards the door.

'If you can't get used to me being in the team,' Jake called after him, 'you'd better go and play for someone else yourself, Ryan. Because I'm not going anywhere.'

Ryan didn't look back. He just carried on walking.

Jake felt his heart beating like a drum. He couldn't believe what he'd just said. And to Ryan. He'd never answered a bully back like that before.

*

The under-twelves were on the training pitches again. The last training session before the big game on Sunday. City away. City: Jake's team.

'Right, lads,' Steve said. 'We're not doing drills this afternoon. We'll go straight into attack and defence. I'm going to split you into two teams.'

Steve pointed at one group of boys. Ryan and the other defenders in the squad.

'I want you lot to defend,' Steve said. 'Ryan, you organize them.'

Then Steve pointed at Jake, Yunis and the group behind him. 'And I want you lot to attack. Jake, you organize that. Let's get some practice in before we play City. I know you'll *all* be keen to beat them.'

Jake smiled to himself as the boys arranged themselves at one end of the pitch. He couldn't wait. City away was his

chance to prove to everyone that he wanted
to be a United player. He looked at Ryan,
but he couldn't catch his eye.

Steve rolled the ball to Jake.

'You're in charge, Jake. I want you to
start every attack. Use the full width of the
pitch. And vary it.'

Jake trapped the ball and looked up. In
front of him was Ryan, still not looking him
in the eye.

Steve blew his whistle.

Jake moved the ball forward and saw immediately that Ryan was approaching him, leaving his central defence position.

Ryan looked determined.

He wants to make his point straight away, Jake thought.

Jake carried on, side-footed the ball to Chi, then sprinted full-pelt, past Ryan. Chi knocked the ball over Ryan right into Jake's path. Jake was running with it now, Ryan beaten.

But forty yards out from goal, he could hear Ryan behind him again. Thirty yards out, Ryan was closer. He was fast and would tackle at any moment.

But Jake was fast too. He took three more strides and hit the ball hard.

Nobody had expected it: most of the defence had moved towards Will and Yunis, who were waiting for a cross into the box. And Tomasz was slightly off his line.

The ball flew, like a bullet, past all the defenders, over Tomasz, dipping into the net.

The first to make it over to Jake was Yunis.

'That was class, Jake,' he said.

As Tomasz pulled the ball out of the goal, Jake looked to the sidelines. Ryan's mum looked furious, but further down the pitch Jake saw his dad standing, nodding quietly to himself and smiling. Jake wanted to see that again. And again and again and again.

The Fall

Jake was the first back to the dressing rooms. At least he thought he was. But then he heard voices coming from inside. Shouting.

Jake stopped and waited in the corridor. He didn't want to interrupt whatever was going on.

'You just let that kid make a fool of you,' the shouting voice continued. 'Why couldn't you get near him?'

It was a woman's voice. Jake knew who it was immediately.

'He's fast,' Ryan said. He sounded quiet. Not his usual loud self at all.

'He made you look *stupid*. I was *ashamed* of you. You'll *never* make it to the first team if you let boys – new boys! – run rings round you like that. I'm getting tired of this, Ryan. Really tired. I'll wait in the car. You have a think about this. How you're letting me down.'

Jake stepped back as Ryan's mum barged past him, scowling.

He could hear the rest of the lads coming over the footbridge, their boots hammering on the wood.

He went into the dressing room.

Ryan was sat in his usual place, his head covered with a towel. When Ryan heard Jake come in, he looked up, his face open and eager.

He thinks I'm his mum coming back, Jake thought. And then he saw that Ryan was crying. His eyes red and swollen. Tears on his face.

They stared at each other for a moment.

The footsteps of the other boys were getting louder. They'd be at the door in a few seconds.

Ryan looked at Jake as if to ask for help.

Jake stepped back into the corridor and

closed the door. Then he fell on the floor and grabbed his ankle.

It took a minute or so for Steve to lift Jake to his feet so he could test his leg.

'Does it hurt?' Steve said.

Jake could see Tomasz and Yunis behind Steve, looking worried. And behind them the rest of the under-twelves' squad.

'I don't think so,' Jake said. 'I just slipped.'

'The floor's wet,' Steve said. 'Can you put some weight on your foot?'

Jake trod carefully, gradually letting go of Steve.

'I think so,' Jake said. 'It's nothing.'

'Just let me get you to the benches,' Steve said.

He led Jake into the dressing rooms. Jake looked to see if Ryan was still there.

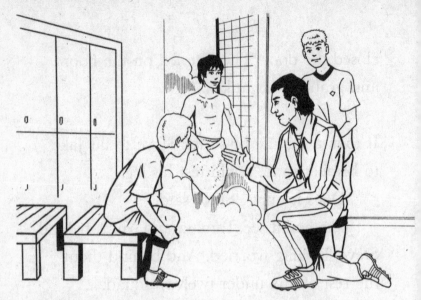

But all he could see was steam from the
shower. As Jake sat down, Ryan came out of
the cubicle. His whole face red from the
shower, covered in drops of water.

'What's up?' Ryan said, looking at Jake
with a blank face. 'Someone hurt?'

Ryan was the first to leave the dressing
rooms. He'd not said a word to Jake. But he
had looked at him. Not smiling. But not
frowning either.

Chi, Will and Yunis were talking about Ryan. They were the last to get changed.

'You've got to feel sorry for him,' Will said. 'His mum's a bit full on. I mean . . . I thought my dad was bad. But she's nuts.'

'He doesn't have to take it out on us, though, does he?' Chi said. 'What do you think, Jake?'

Jake shrugged.

'It's hard,' Will said. 'My dad gets so excited about it. I mean, you remember the trial, Jake? That was embarrassing – when he came into the dressing room and told me I'd got a place.'

'I suppose,' Jake said.

'I'd be happy if my dad took that much interest,' Yunis added.

Jake put his head down. He felt glad his dad was just normal. He remembered how Dad had said nothing when they went to

talk to Steve. His dad was supporting him:
but left him to it.

Jake pulled his shoes on and stood up.

'Right. I'm off. I'll see you at the City
game.'

City v United

Match day. Five minutes before kick-off. City versus United.

Jake was talking to a boy he knew in the City team when Ryan came up behind him. Zack was one of City's best players – tall, blond and a really good striker. Jake had played with him in teams before. Both City fans, they'd been brought up in the same village.

Ryan put his arm round Jake. 'Which top are you wearing today, City fan?'

'Same as you, Ryan,' Jake said.

'I hope so,' Ryan said.

'Give me the ball and I'll prove it,' Jake offered.

Jake noticed Zack looking confused, like he wanted to ask what was happening.

'Have you *got* your City top with you?' Ryan said.

'Drop it, Ryan,' Jake replied. 'No, I haven't got my City top with me. Yes, I am a United player. What else do you want me to tell you?'

Ryan walked off, leaving Jake to talk to Zack. Jake wondered if Ryan was going to be even worse with him, now Jake had seen him crying.

It was a strange day. Jake had to admit that. The minute he'd entered the City ground he'd felt it. This was the home of the team he had always supported. The team whose shirt he always had in his bag for luck. But, like he'd told Ryan, he didn't have his City shirt with him today. It was at home on his bed. He'd left it there for once. He wasn't sure why.

But that didn't matter. What mattered was today and what he did in his United shirt.

United were strong from the kick-off. They attacked for the first ten minutes, with City barely getting a look-in. And Ryan was playing the ball wide to *both* wings, including Jake.

Jake was happy with what he'd done so far. He was playing well, now he was getting the ball. He was starting to prove he really was a United player.

The first real chance for United to take the lead came after twelve minutes. Jake took the ball wide, then passed it to Ryan in the centre circle, who switched it to the right side and Ben.

Jake ran into the six-yard area, expecting a cross. But Ben crossed it to Yunis who was near the penalty spot. Yunis controlled the ball and shot quickly. The ball flew towards the goal, heading straight for the bottom right corner. Jake saw it coming. He jumped to get out of the way. But the ball hit him on the ankle and spun wide.

Jake had stopped it going in, stopped his own team from scoring.

Yunis grinned at Jake, thinking it was funny. He came over. 'Don't worry, Jake. It was an accident. Just don't do it next time I shoot.'

Then Zack ran past Jake and ruffled his hair. 'Cheers, mate.'

Jake shrugged it off. He looked at Steve, who was encouraging the team to get back and defend.

As they were running back though, Ryan shouted at Jake. 'Nice block, Jake. I *said* you were a City player.'

Jake heard some of the parents on the sidelines laughing.

He felt really angry. But this time, instead of it making him question himself, it made him all the more determined to prove Ryan wrong.

United

Ryan brought the ball forward, as
usual, after United had won back
possession. The City defence was
backing off again.

Jake wondered how long it was going to
take for him to get an opportunity to
redeem himself. He was desperate to make
up for his mistake.

His chance came five minutes later.
Ryan was about to play the ball to Ben, but
then seemed to change his mind.

Ryan looked up. Jake had run into the space right in front of Ryan, whereas Ben was being marked closely by two defenders. Ryan knocked it to Jake. Jake immediately spun and ran at the City defence without giving them time to think. He wrong-footed the first defender, then, with players all around him, played the ball back to Ryan, who had come forward to support the attack.

He was really happy that it was Ryan

he'd been able to pass it to. The more they played like this, the better things would be.

Jake ran towards the penalty box. Ryan had four players he could pass to. Ben on the left. Yunis and Jake on the edge of the box. And Will alongside him. To Jake's surprise, Ryan lobbed the ball forward to him in the box.

Something had changed. Definitely.

Surprised, but pleased, Jake leaped high enough to head the ball down to Yunis, who was making a run into the box.

Yunis belted the ball home.

The net bulged. The City keeper had no chance.

One–nil.

After congratulating Yunis, Ryan jogged over to Jake and patted him on the back.

'Good header, Jake.'

'You made it with that chip,' Jake said.

And Jake saw Ryan grin.

From then on the game went well. Jake was getting more space out wide – and more of the ball from Ryan. United were putting an attack together every minute, threatening to score more goals.

And at the other end Tomasz pulled off two great saves to keep United ahead.

Jake's new confidence meant that he was happy to take on defenders. Using his pace and skill, he beat them again and again, sending crosses into the box. Yunis managed to get on the end of two of the crosses, to complete a hat-trick.

This reminded Jake of the trial. Him and Yunis. The Deadly Duo.

Then – with a few minutes left – Jake took the ball wide again. As he did, he

noticed Ryan moving up from the defence.
Jake decided to try and set Ryan up with a
goal. He drew the City defender towards
the corner flag. Then he beat him and ran
into the penalty box.

Ryan was on the far side of the penalty
box, a forest of players between them. So
Jake pretended to shoot, making all the
defenders move towards the goal to try and
block it.

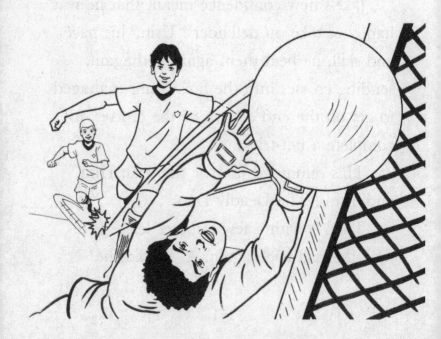

But – at the last minute – Jake played the ball across the area to Ryan, in the gap made by the defenders. Ryan had all the time in the world to blast the ball home.

City 0 United 4. And Jake had set them all up.

In the car on the way home, Dad was quiet. All he'd done when he met up with Jake after the game was give him a big hug. And that was all Jake needed.

As Dad drove through the city, Jake was thinking of the crosses he'd put over to Yunis; the pats on the back from Ryan; and the handshake he'd got from Steve at the end of the game.

What had Steve said?

'Whatever you had for your breakfast, have it next week. That was brilliant, Jake.

You were definitely my man of the match. Even if Yunis did score three.'

Jake sat back in the seat and smiled, his eyes closed.

'That smile will crack your face open if it gets any wider, Jake,' Dad said.

Then, after a few seconds, Jake said, 'Thanks, Dad.'

Dad looked puzzled. 'What for?'

'For helping me. I was thinking about packing it in.'

'Don't mention it,' Dad said. 'I think we should celebrate. How about a pizza and a film?'

'I've got a better idea,' Jake said. 'How about a kick about on the fields, tonight? When we get back. Just you and me.'

'Great,' Dad said.

'*Then* the pizza and the film,' Jake said, laughing.

Sunday 9 October
City 0 United 4
Goals: Yunis (3), Ryan
Bookings: none

Under-twelves manager's marks out of ten for each player:

Tomasz	7
Connor	7
James	8
Ryan	8
Ronan	6
Chi	7
Sam	6
Will	6
Jake	9
Yunis	9
Ben	6

Thank Yous

The Football Academy series came about thanks
to the imagination and hard work of Sarah
Hughes, Alison Dougal and Helen Levene at
Puffin, working with David Luxton at Luxton
Harris Literary Agency. Thanks are due to all four
for giving me this opportunity: thank you! Thanks
also to Wendy Tse for all her hard work with the
fine detail, and to everyone at Puffin for all they
do, including Reetu Kabra, Adele Minchin, Louise
Heskett, Sarah Kettle, Tom Sanderson and the
rights team. Thanks also to Brian Williamson for
the great cover image and illustrations.

I needed a lot of help to make sure the
academy at 'United' was as close to an English

football club's academy as possible. Burnley Football Club let me come to training and matches at their Gawthorpe Hall training ground to watch the under-twelves. Vince Overson and Jeff Taylor gave me lots of time at Burnley and I am extremely grateful. I was also given excellent advice by Kit Carson and Steve Cooper.

Ralph Newbrook at the Football Foundation gave me loads of advice and read the finished manuscript. He – more than anyone – has helped me make this book and series more realistic. Thank you, Ralph!

Thanks also to Nikki Woodman for her excellent comments on the book as it developed and Daniel Taylor for his very useful reading too.

Huge thanks to my writing group in Leeds – James Nash and Sophie Hannah. Our mornings drinking coffee have been an enormous help.

Mostly though, thank you to my wife, Rebecca, and daughter, Iris, who have always supported my desire to be a writer, and given me the time and space and confidence to do it.